Jakki Wood studied graphic design at Wolverhampton Polytechnic.
She has illustrated many children's books for Frances Lincoln, including the
Animal Friends series (with Donna Bryant), *Fiddle-I-Fee, Bumper to Bumper,*
The Deep Blue Sea, and three exuberant animal books – *Animal Parade,*
Number Parade and *Animal Hullabaloo.*

"Jakki Wood's lively information books are ideal for stimulating
young children's interest in using books to find out about the world
and about words." *Primary English*

JURASSIC PERIOD
Early Jurassic

Stenopterygius

Cryptoclidus

Plesiosaurus

Scutellosaurus

Scelidosaurus

220 mya

175 mya

Late Jurassic

Rhamphorhynchus

Batrachognathus

Pterodactylus

Ichthyosaurus

160 mya

Coelurus

Allosaurus

Ceratosaurus

Diplodocus

150 mya

Megalosaurus

Ultrasauros

Stegosaurus

Dacentrurus

140 mya

CRETACEOUS PERIOD
Early Cretaceous

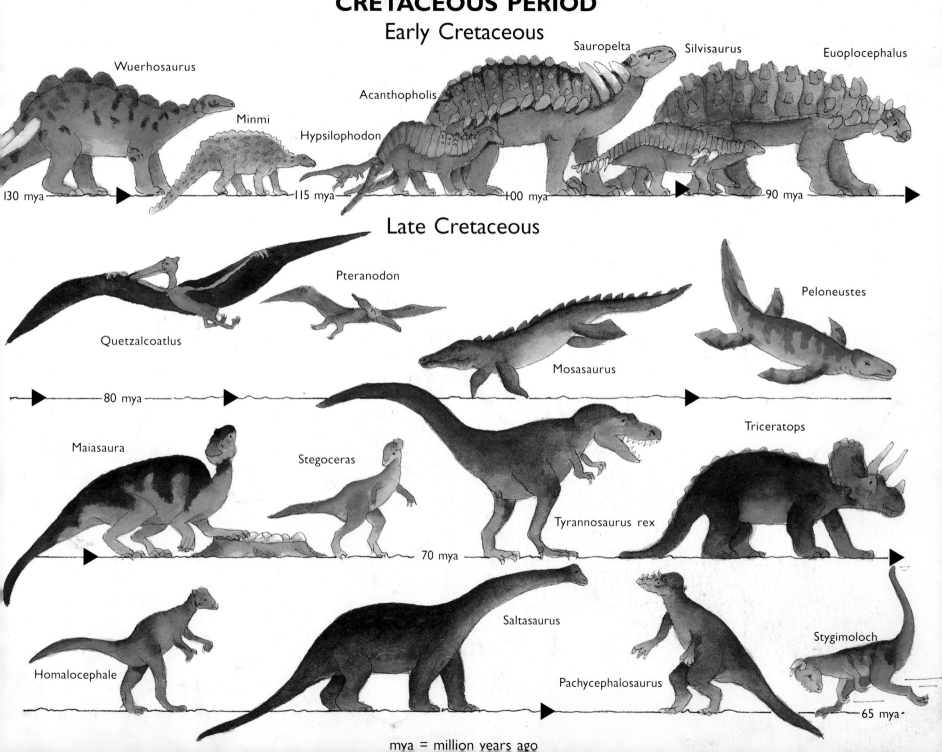

Wuerhosaurus

Minmi

Hypsilophodon

Acantholis

Sauropelta

Silvisaurus

Euoplocephalus

130 mya ▶ 115 mya 100 mya ▶ 90 mya ▶

Late Cretaceous

Quetzalcoatlus

Pteranodon

Mosasaurus

Peloneustes

▶ 80 mya ▶ ▶

Maiasaura

Stegoceras

Tyrannosaurus rex

Triceratops

▶ 70 mya ▶

Homalocephale

Saltasaurus

Pachycephalosaurus

Stygimoloch

▶ 65 mya

mya = million years ago

To Rachel Ann

First published in Great Britain in 1999 by
Frances Lincoln Limited, 4 Torriano Mews
Torriano Avenue, London NW5 2RZ

First paperback edition 2000

The author and publishers would like to thank John A. Cooper, BSc, AMA, FGS,
Keeper of The Booth Museum of Natural History, Brighton, for his help.

British Library Cataloguing in Publication Data
available on request
ISBN   0-7112-1421-2 hardback
        0-7112-1456-5 paperback

Set in Gill Sans

Printed in Hong Kong

9 8 7 6 5 4 3 2

MARCH OF THE DINOSAURS

A Prehistoric Counting Book

Jakki Wood

FRANCES LINCOLN

ultrasauros
ul-tra-**saw**-rus

1 one huge, gigantic, colossal dinosaur

coelurus
seel-**yoo**-rus

two tiny but terrible, hurrying hunters

allosaurus
al-oh-**saw**-rus

megalosaurus
meg-al-oh-**saw**-rus

ceratosaurus
ser-at-oh-**saw**-rus

3 three thrashing, claw-slashing me **2**

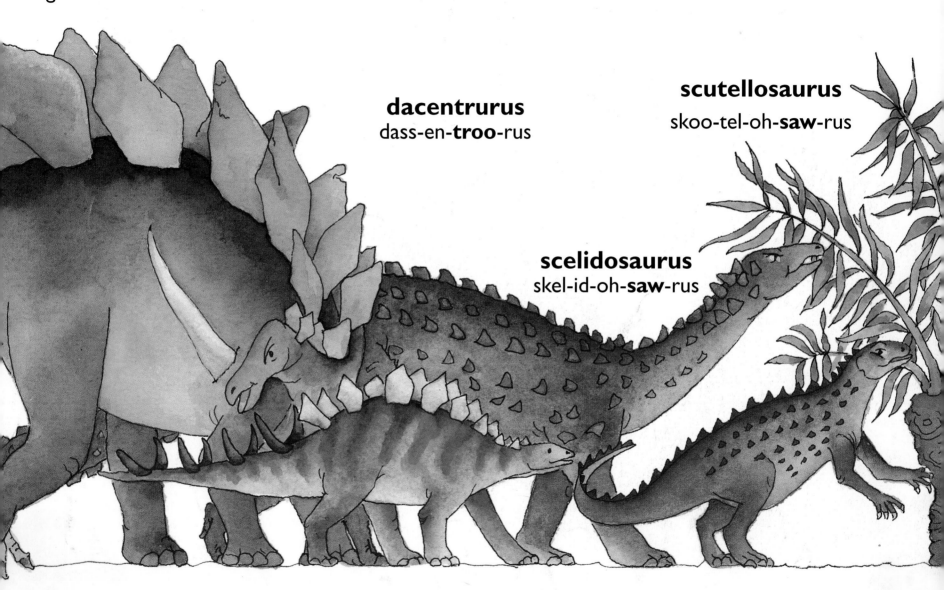

stegosaurus
steg-oh-**saw**-rus

dacentrurus
dass-en-**troo**-rus

scutellosaurus
skoo-tel-oh-**saw**-rus

scelidosaurus
skel-id-oh-**saw**-rus

4 four spiny, scaly, scary tail-thumpers

rhamphorhynchus
ram-for-**rink**-us

pterodactylus
tair-oh-**dak**-til-us

batrachognathus
ba-tra-kog-**nay**-thus

5 five swooping, gliding,

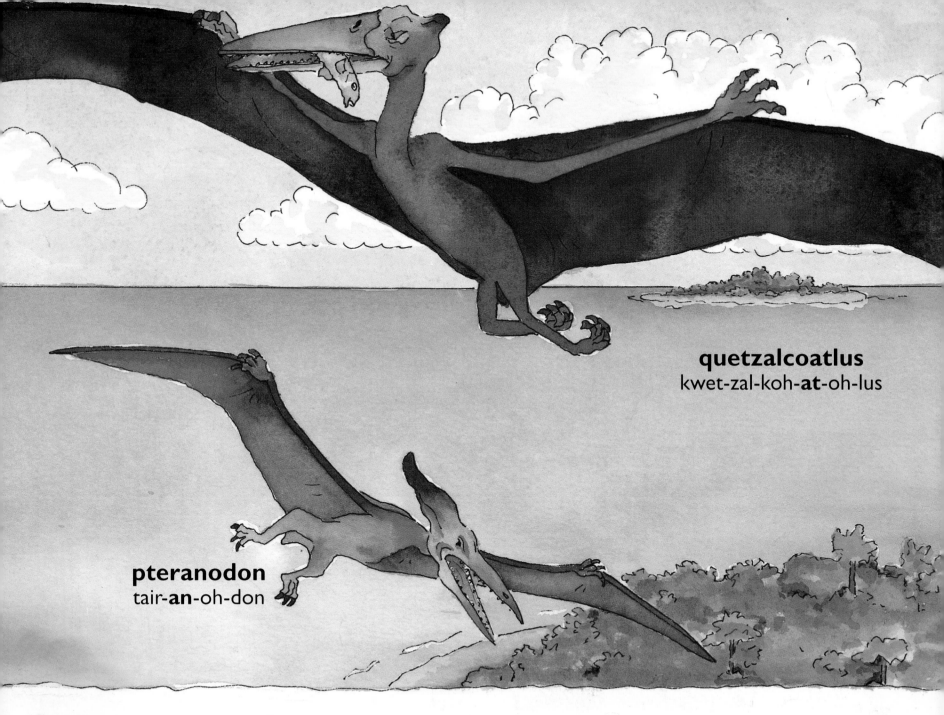

quetzalcoatlus
kwet-zal-koh-**at**-oh-lus

pteranodon
tair-**an**-oh-don

fish-eating fliers

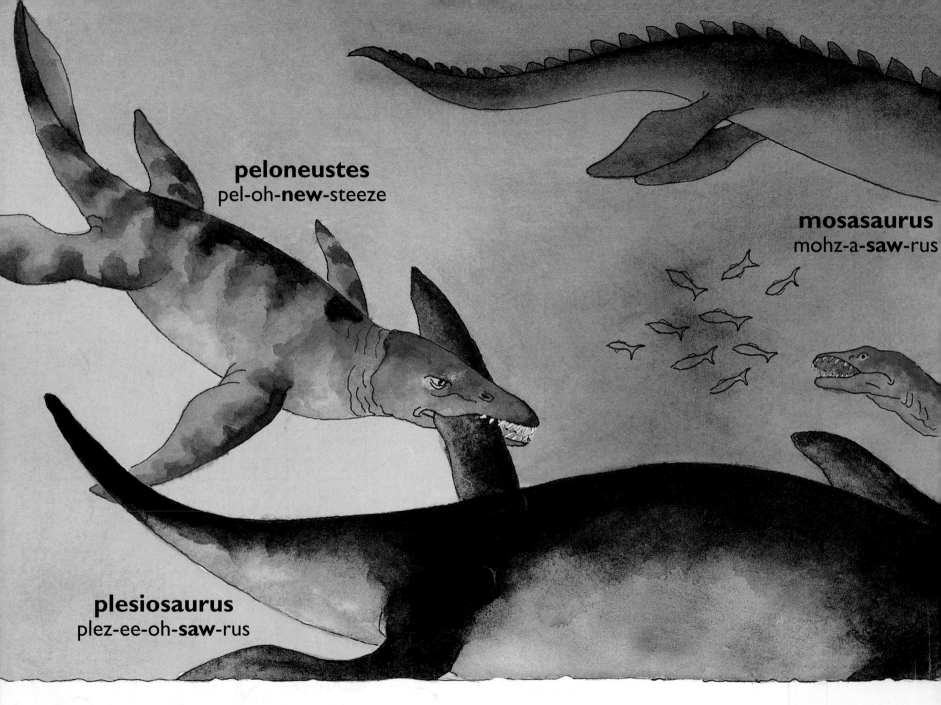

peloneustes
pel-oh-**new**-steeze

mosasaurus
mohz-a-**saw**-rus

plesiosaurus
plez-ee-oh-**saw**-rus

6 six strong, streamlined, savage swimmers

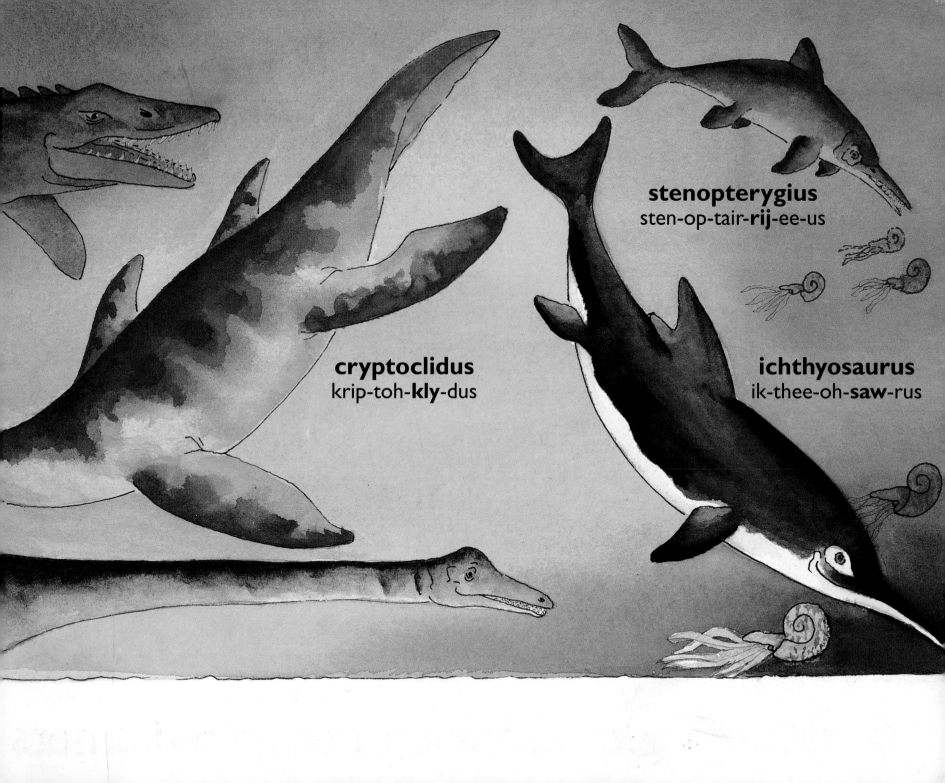

stenopterygius
sten-op-tair-**rij**-ee-us

cryptoclidus
krip-toh-**kly**-dus

ichthyosaurus
ik-thee-oh-**saw**-rus

7 seven solid, slowly strolling, ponderous,

diplodocus
dip-**lod**-oh-kus

long-necked browsers

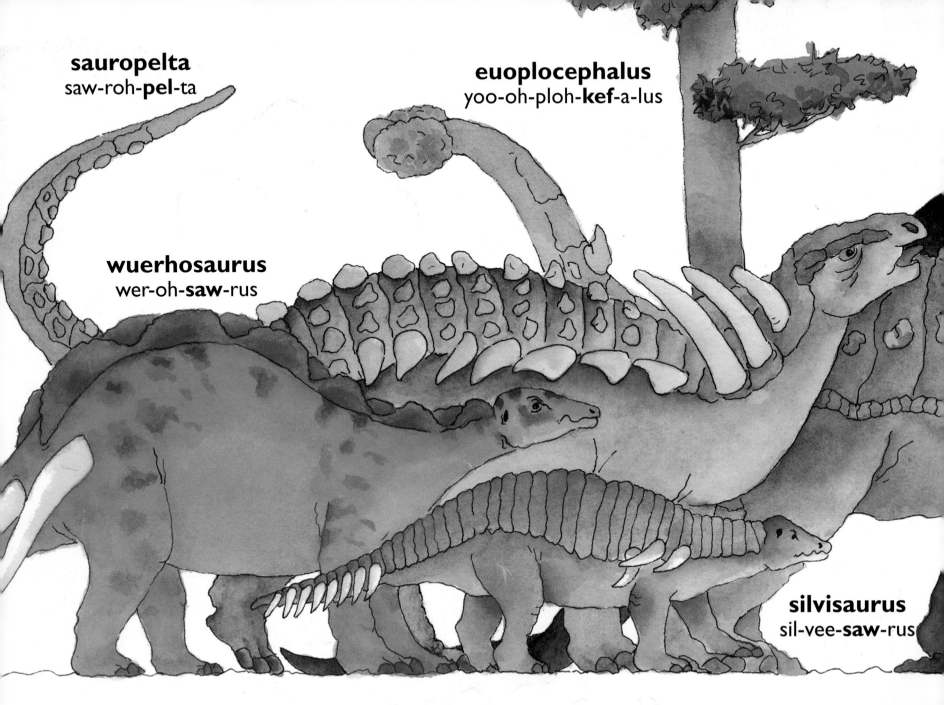

sauropelta
saw-roh-**pel**-ta

euoplocephalus
yoo-oh-ploh-**kef**-a-lus

wuerhosaurus
wer-oh-**saw**-rus

silvisaurus
sil-vee-**saw**-rus

8 eight heavy, armour-plated, crashing,

saltasaurus
salt-a-**saw**-rus

triceratops
try-**ser**-a-tops

minmi
min-mee

acanthopholis
a-kan-thoh-**fohl**-is

tail-lashing lumberers

pachycephalosaurus
pak-ee-kef-al-oh-**saw**-rus

stegoceras
steg-**oss**-e-ras

9 nine rough, rampant, raging,

homalocephale
hom-al-oh-**sef**-a-lee

stygimoloch
stij-ee-**mol**-ok

battering head-bangers

tyrannosaurus rex
ty-ran-oh-**saw**-rus rex

10 ten tall, terrifying, roaring, clawing,

furious, flesh-tearing bone-crushers

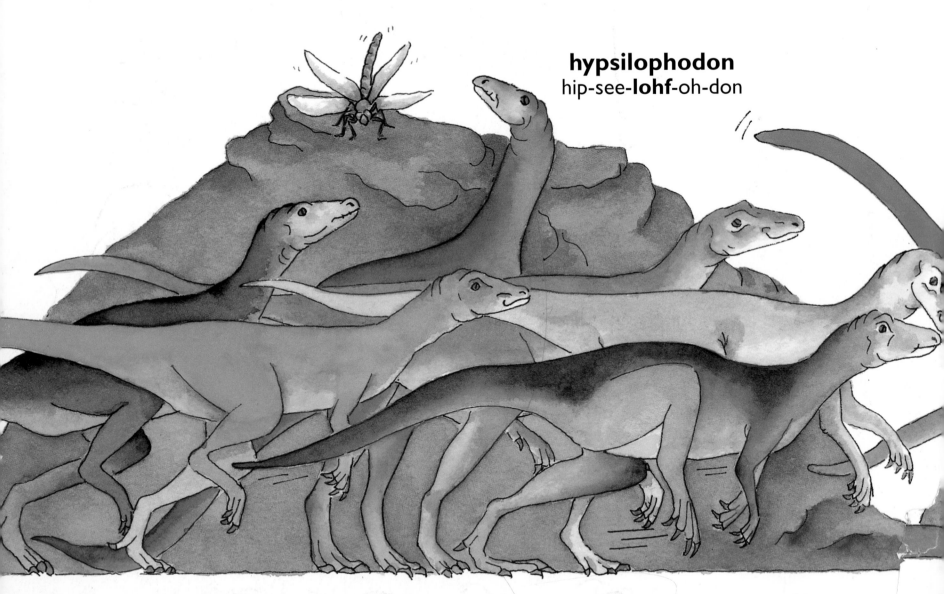

hypsilophodon
hip-see-**lohf**-oh-don

11 eleven lively, hurry-scurry,

sharp-toothed, trip-trotting racers

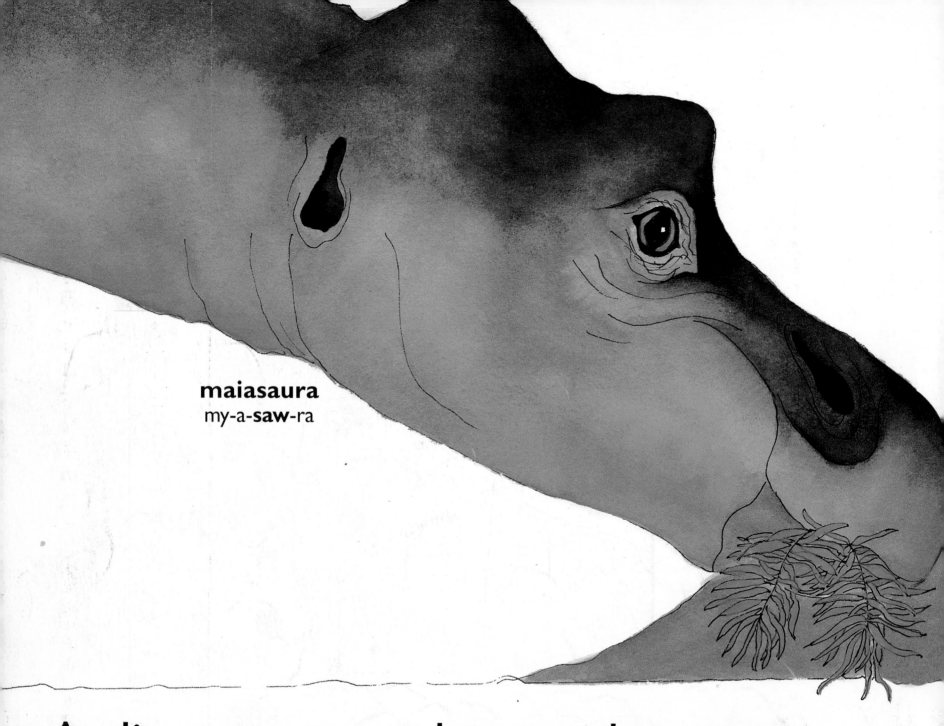

maiasaura
my-a-**saw**-ra

A dinosaur mum lays twelve eggs.

How many creatures can you name?

MORE PICTURE BOOKS IN PAPERBACK BY JAKKI WOOD
PUBLISHED BY FRANCES LINCOLN

FIDDLE-I-FEE

An exuberant retelling of a well-known nursery rhyme that will have children singing along in no time.
Margaret Lion has arranged the accompanying melody, based on a traditional folk song, for piano and guitar.

Suitable for National Curriculum English - Key Stage 1

Scottish Guidelines English Language - Reading, Level A

ISBN 0-7112-0860-3   £4.99

ANIMAL PARADE

Featuring a nose-to-tail march-past of 95 spectacular species, from Aardvark to Zebra.
Never has the ABC been such an adventure!

Suitable for National Curriculum English - Reading, Key Stage 1

Scottish Guidelines English Language - Reading, Level A

ISBN 0-7112-0777-1   £4.99

ANIMAL HULLABALOO

From dawn chorus to night-time call, more than 80 birds, beasts and reptiles raise their voices in
animated uproar, with a glorious hullabaloo of sounds children will love to imitate.

Suitable for National Curriculum English - Reading, Key Stage 1

Scottish Guidelines English Language - Reading, Level A

ISBN 0-7112-0946-4   £4.99

BUMPER TO BUMPER

In the busiest, liveliest, most enormous traffic jam you've ever seen,
identify and learn the names of more than 20 vehicles.

Suitable for National Curriculum - Nursery Level

Scottish Guidelines English Language - Nursery Level

ISBN 0-7112-1031-4   £4.99

Frances Lincoln titles are available from all good bookshops.
Prices are correct at time of publication, but may be subject to change.